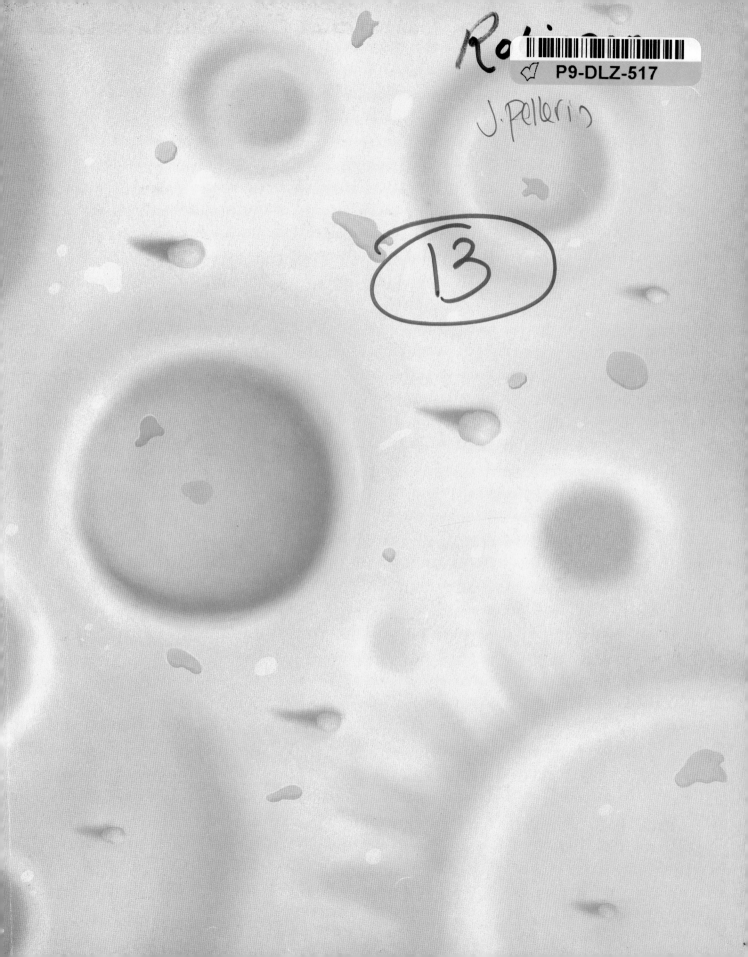

9/11/01

MOONDOGS

Daniel
Kirk

G. P. Putnam's Sons
New York

For my explorers,
Raleigh and Russell

The author wishes to thank Anthony Priolo and his dog Casey.

Printed in Hong Kong by South China Printing Co. (1988) Ltd.
Designed by Julia Gorton. Text set in Template Gothic
The artwork in this book was prepared using oil paint on paper.

Library of Congress Cataloging-in-Publication Data
Kirk, Daniel. Moondogs / Daniel Kirk. p. cm.
Summary: Willy flies to the moon to get a moondog for a pet, but he finds true happiness
with a scruffy but loyal Earth dog named Scrappy. [1. Dogs—Fiction. 2. Moon—Fiction.
3. Stories in rhyme.] I. Title. PZ8.3.K6553Mo 1999 [E]—dc21 98-15521 CIP AC
ISBN 0-399-23128-5
1 3 5 7 9 10 8 6 4 2
First Impression

On a clear and pleasant evening in the early part of June, young Willy Joe Jehosephat stood gazing at the moon.

"Someday," said his mother,
"he'll be an astronaut, I bet;
but there's more to life
than stars and space—
he needs a pal, a pet!"

"You're spending too
much time alone,"
his father said next day.
"Let's go and buy a dog,
and then the two of
you can play!"

Will said,
"I'd like to get a moondog—
that's the perfect pet for me.
I watch them through my telescope.
They're real, I guarantee!"

Will went out to the garage
to build a rocket just his size.
"When I get back," he said,
"my dad is in for a surprise!"

With a flash of light
the spaceship soared.
"Moonward ho!" Will said.
"I'll pick the perfect
moondog and be home in
time for bed!"

Stars whizzed past the windows.

Willy went to get his snack,

but found a mangy mongrel busy digging in his pack!

"That food was mine," Will grumbled,
"but you're scrappy, and so thin!

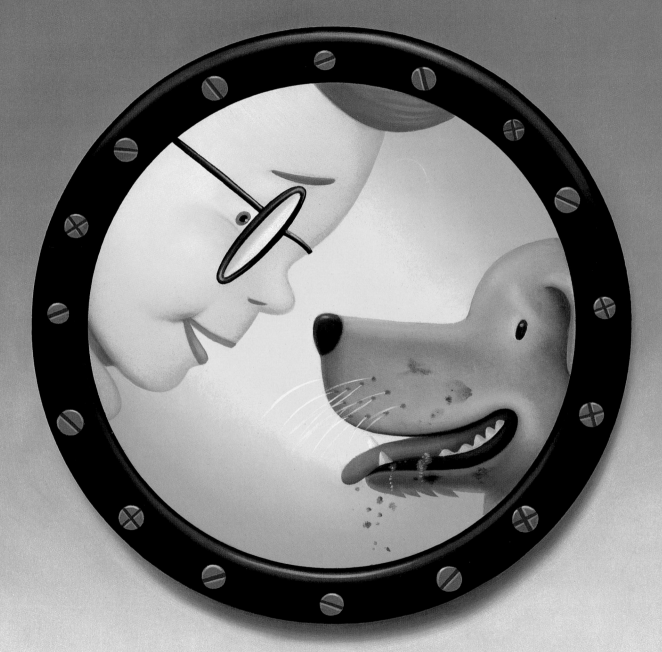

I'll ask the moondogs what to do—
perhaps they'll take you in."

Just then they reached the moon.
Will's rocket skidded to a stop.
He pulled his homemade helmet on,
got out, and climbed on top!

"I'm Will", he called,
"I come from Earth,
in case you hadn't guessed.
My dad thinks I should get a dog,
and moondogs are the best!"

Then angry footsteps
shook the ground;

a shadow blocked the sun.

The man in the moon came crashing in

and made the moondogs run!

"I've got you now,"
the moon man growled.
His breath was hot and sour.
"Each noisy boy or dog I catch,
I'm going to devour!"

Then Scrappy, loyal earth dog,
bounded in to join the fight.
He jumped and chomped
the moon man's leg
with one ferocious bite!

The moon man fled, but left his pants.
He knew he'd met his match.
Scrappy growled contentedly,
and settled down to scratch.

Will gazed around the crater
with a shy and guilty grin;
"I owe my life to Scrappy—
   he's the dog who saved my skin!"
"What courage!"
   all the moondogs crooned,
"Forgive us if we're wrong,
   but Will, the pet you ought to have
was with you all along!"

Will gave the moondogs good-bye hugs,
then climbed beneath the dome.
"You'll love my mom and dad," he said.
"Come on, we're going home!"

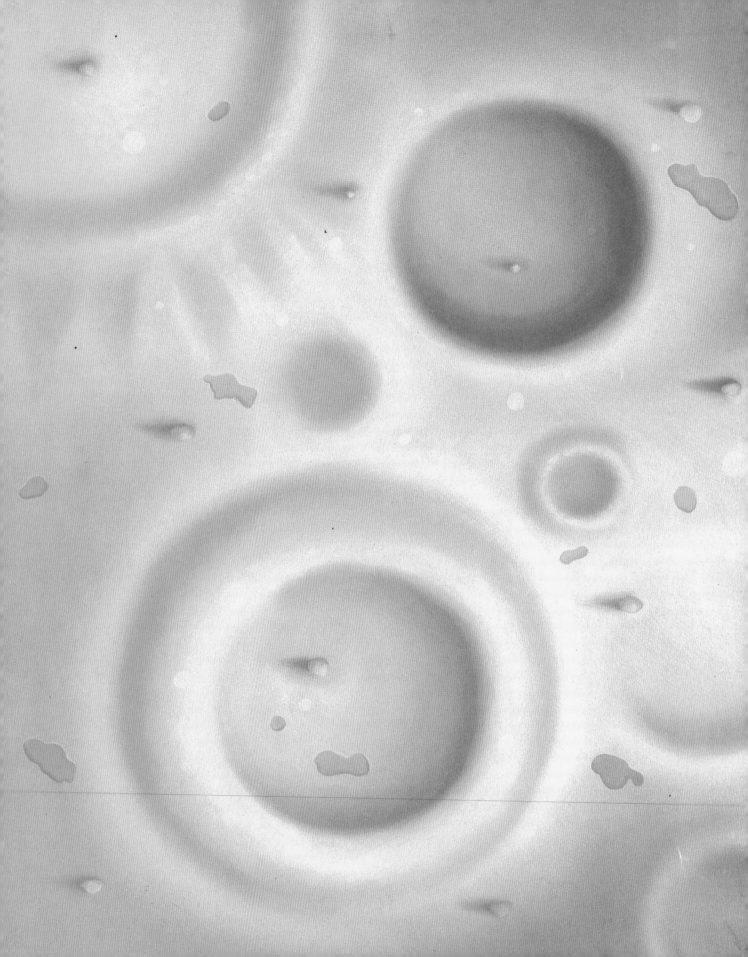